I ESCAPED THE HAUNTED WINCHESTER HOUSE

A HAUNTED HOUSE SURVIVAL STORY

ELLIE CROWE

SCOTT PETERS

I Escaped The Haunted Winchester House (I Escaped #10)

ISBN: 978-1-951019-31-0 (Hardcover)

ISBN: 978-1-951019-30-3 (Paperback)

While inspired by real events, this is a work of fiction and does not claim to be historically accurate or portray factual events or relationships. References to historical events, real persons, business establishments and real places are used fictitiously and may not be factually accurate, but rather fictionalized by the author.

Cover design by Susan Wyshynski

Best Day Books For Young Readers

I ESCAPED THE HAUNTED WINCHESTER HOUSE

CHAPTER 1

It was almost midnight. Dark shadows filled every corner of the Winchester House Ballroom, and ghostly fog swirled.

Fifteen-year-old Jesse peered into the gloom. His blue eyes flared in shock. There, across the empty floor, a figure was materializing.

Yikes!

A tall, thin man wavered, ghost-like, fading in and out. He stared at Jesse, his hair writhing like squiggly octopus tentacles.

1

"I see something," Jesse whispered, trying to keep his voice steady.

At his back, his fifteen-year-old cousin, Emma, stiffened.

"What sort of thing?" she whispered.

"A weird thing. Look! Over there." Jesse pointed.

Emma's bushy hair tickled his nose as she peeked over his shoulder. "Eek, what is that?"

"Might be a spirit. I've got to get a picture."

"Take it fast and let's go," she hissed.

Jesse set the Kodak Brownie on a rickety table and opened the shutter.

"Hurry up!" Emma hissed. "It's moving this way."

A sudden shriek broke the silence. A small boy with wild, curly hair charged across the ballroom, nearly knocking over the camera.

Emma made a futile grab for her nephew. "GL!" she called after the retreating boy. "Get back here!"

Jesse groaned. "So much for my shot. I can't believe you brought him."

"GL," Emma shouted, "Where are you going?"

Jesse snatched up his camera, slung it around his neck, and raced after GL. Good old Sniffer, Jesse's black Labrador, galloped alongside, his tongue hanging out.

The house creaked and moaned.

GL reached the corridor's far end and clambered up a steep, narrow stairway. At the top, he scrambled crab-like onto a landing. Jesse grabbed the kid's ankle, stopping him dead. GL's floppy blue hat flew over the wooden railing. It spun into the pool of darkness below.

"My hat!" GL yelled.

"Shh!" Emma gasped, catching up. "Someone's coming. Hide!"

Sniffer let out a low whine.

"Good boy, it's okay," Jesse whispered.

Footsteps—shuffling footsteps—scratched along the hallway. Slow and steady, heading in their direction.

Then, an angry moan shook the walls. A horrible shriek followed.

Eyes bugging out, Jesse stared at the space where a person should be. There was no one there!

This wasn't good. How did you run from something you couldn't see?

"Through here," he said, pointing at one of the many oak doors lining the corridor.

Emma tried the handle. "Locked."

Jesse grabbed another brass doorknob. "Locked, too."

Emma wrapped a protective arm around GL. Her pointed face was ashen with fear. "I told you this was a bad idea."

"What about this room?" Jesse reached for a third doorknob, but as he grabbed it, the knob began to rattle and turn. "That's not me doing that."

"Then who is?" Emma said.

Someone, or *something*.

Jesse snatched his hand away as though the knob was red hot.

You're grounded. I hope you think long and hard about what you said."

"But it's Saturday night. And it was Pete's fault! Why don't you believe me? You never believe me."

Dressed in a tight, white undershirt, Pete leaned against Jesse's bedroom wall, his arms folded across his bulging chest. He flashed Jesse a shark-like grin from behind Dad's back. Nineteen years old, he always got off scot-free.

Why couldn't Dad back Jesse up just once?

Worst of all, Jesse had big plans for tonight. He and his cousin Emma were supposed to sneak into the haunted Winchester House. Looks like he'd be stuck in his room instead.

"You're never fair." Jesse stared at the floor.

"Is that what you think?" Dad said in that low voice that meant trouble. "Based on what? Why don't you give me an example?"

Jessie hated when Dad acted like he was some sort of expert interrogator, trying to trap him up, trying to find a crack in his story.

"Based on right now." At once, Jesse realized it was a dumb thing to say.

"Right, if that's how you choose to speak to me, you can spend the whole weekend in your room. And when you get out, you can apologize to Pete for calling him names and to me for lack of respect."

Jesse opened his mouth to backtrack.

Dad said, "Not another peep." He left without waiting for a reply.

Gee whiz. What a dictator.

Pete grinned like a cat with a canary. His white teeth flashed in his suntanned face. "Loser!"

"Takes one to know one."

Pete stretched, showing off his famous pitcher forearms. "Enjoy your weekend." He sauntered off.

From downstairs, Dad shouted, "And clean your room. The place looks like a pigsty."

Jesse took quick stock of his bedroom. It looked like it always did—like a bomb had blown apart his closet. Okay, Dad had him there.

Still, at least the walls looked good. He'd tacked up some great posters from the amazing 1904 St. Louis World's Fair.

He studied one of his favorites: a dripping waffle ice-cream cone. Looked yummy. Ice cream cones had been invented right at the St. Louis World's Fair. He admired his other great posters: the giant ferris wheel, dinosaur skeletons, an elephant made of almonds, the massive clown on the Temple of Mirth, the Asian dancers, the African Pygmies.

What fun it would be to ride in a hot air balloon like a photojournalist, taking pictures at the World's Fair. Photojournalists did some great stuff. When he finished college, that's what he wanted to be.

He'd planned to start his new career tonight by taking pictures inside the Winchester House, the weirdest house in America. He hoped he could even get a photo in the paper. That was off, now, though.

Frustrated, he flopped onto his bed, legs dangling. Pete never got punished. He knew how to get around Dad. Because, like Dad before him, Pete had made star pitcher on the San Jose High School's baseball team. His fastballs had hit eighty-five. And every time he scored a strike-out, Dad yelled, "Way to go, son!"

Also, Pete was a crack shot with Gramp's Winchester hunting rifle.

Dad treasured that hunting rifle because Gramps helped design it. He'd told them a million times how famous it was—*The Gun That Won the West*. Dad thought it was a supreme honor when he allowed Pete and Jesse to take it hunting.

But Jesse wasn't a great shot. Not even a good shot.

Whenever they headed to Suisun Marsh for a day of wildfowl hunting, Pete brought down at least two flying geese, one for dinner and one that Mom would preserve for later.

Every time, Dad cheered, "Well done, son! Way to go, Pete!"

Jesse had never brought down a flying goose in his

life. Not even when great flocks filled the sky. He missed every one.

Pete called him blind as a bat. Of course, Pete never got into trouble for saying that.

It wasn't Jesse's fault for being nearsighted. He rubbed his eyes, annoyed at the unfairness.

"No way am I staying in my room tonight," he muttered. "I'm sneaking into that spooky Winchester House no matter what. I've been planning this for weeks. I'm going to borrow Dad's Kodak Brownie and take pictures of the weirdest stuff I can find. I'll be the first one to take pictures in there, and no one's going to stop me. And when I get my pictures in the paper, even Dad and Pete will be impressed."

CHAPTER 3

Jesse's home
2 minutes later

Jesse stood staring out his bedroom window, mulling over his plans. Dark clouds massed on the horizon, and the dry trees stood like skeletons, their brittle limbs rattling in the wind.

Across the fields, he could just make out the Winchester House's gothic-looking turrets and domes.

What a weird place. Seven stories high! And tonight, all one-hundred-and-sixty rooms and miles of zig-zagging hallways were empty. Dad was the building foreman, and he said Sarah Winchester was out of town. The builders, who normally worked day-and-night around the clock building the place, had been given a break.

It was the perfect night to sneak in. Jesse could hardly wait.

Emma, on the other hand, wasn't quite so keen. Still, she'd said yes, adding that he'd need her brains in case he got into trouble. He grinned. She'd been joking, but she'd gotten them out of a few jams in the past. He tended to charge into things full-speed ahead, which didn't always end well. She, on the other hand, liked to puzzle things out first.

Anyway, as long as they weren't chased by angry spirits, they'd be fine. He didn't *actually* believe the stories—that ghosts haunted the house because they were angry at the family who invented the Winchester repeating rifles.

According to Dad, though, Sarah Winchester believed it. She thought they wanted to kill her and take their revenge on her family. That's why Mrs. Winchester kept building so many rooms, halls, and stairwells, to confuse the spirits so they couldn't find her. She even slept in a different bedroom each night to escape them!

A breeze sent a brown, leathery leaf skittering through his open window. It twirled toward his face, making him jump back. As he swatted it aside, a loud crack made his heart stutter. Was that a rifle?

No, just a branch breaking in the wind.

Something shuffled under his bed, and he turned quickly.

Sniffer, Jesse's black lab, stuck out his nose. Sniffer didn't like it when Dad yelled.

Jesse let out the breath he didn't know he'd been holding. "Hey, boy. Ready for a big adventure?"

Sniffer cocked his head.

"At the Winchester House?"

Sniffer responded with a low whine, tucking his chin between his paws. Usually, Sniffer was up for action. Tonight, he didn't seem into it.

"It'll be neat, Sniffer, I promise."

As long as they didn't get caught. Otherwise, he'd be grounded for the rest of the year.

He ran his fingers through his cropped brown hair. He'd have to wait until Mom and Dad were asleep—after eleven at least. He just hoped Emma would still be up for it. He didn't like the idea of going alone. Only one way to find out.

He tiptoed down the hall. Mom and Dad's voices echoed from the kitchen. Pete was nowhere in sight.

Jesse made a silent sprint for the small table that held

the family telephone and snatched up the handset.

"Number, please," the operator said.

"One, four, two, six," Jesse said.

"Trying now."

Emma answered on the fifth ring.

Low and quick, Jesse whispered, "Change of plans. I can't get out till eleven. Let's meet at that wrought-iron front gate in front of the Winchester House. At five after."

"What?" Emma said. "I can't hear you."

Jesse winced. Next thing, Dad or Pete would come looking to see who he was talking to. He spoke slightly louder. "The Winchester House plan is on. But we're going later. Meet me at the gate at five after eleven."

"Still can't hear you," Emma said.

From her end came a noise like a siren going off. "What's that racket?"

"It's GL," Emma said. "My nephew."

"Gotcha." Checking to make sure the coast was clear, Jesse spoke louder. "Meet me at the Winchester House front gate at eleven-oh-five."

There was a rustle on the phone line. That wasn't good. Was the nosy operator listening in? Or one of the neighbors on the party line?

"Eleven? That late?" Emma said.

"Has to be. I'll explain later."

Emma was silent a moment. "I don't think we should," she said. "If our parents find out, we're dead. And what if it really is haunted? And there's a storm coming. Besides, it'll be dark in that huge, creepy place. We said we'd go before sunset."

Jesse took a deep breath. Emma was going to back

13

out. "If we get in there, we'll be famous," he said. "Our names will go down in school history."

"How?" Emma said. "No one will believe us."

"They will. Because here's the thing. I'm borrowing Dad's Kodak Brownie camera. Come on, you have to help me. You know how bad I want to be a photographer, and this is my best chance. Please? I need your brains in case I get into trouble, remember?"

Long pause.

"Your dad will kill you for borrowing it without asking," Emma said.

True. But Jesse ignored the warning. "Wait till we show Pete the pictures. He'll be green with envy. Remember last year when Pete and his girlfriend tried to sneak into the house on Halloween? And got caught by that handyman? My brother's still never been in there."

"Yeah." Emma laughed. "For once, we'd be the top dogs. Instead of Pete always showing everyone up."

"It's the only night the place will be empty."

"I'll think about it," she said.

"I'll be waiting at five after. Please don't let me down, Emma!"

CHAPTER 4

JESSE'S HOME

J esse slid the telephone handset back into its holder.

He had to grab Dad's Kodak Brownie camera out of the living room cabinet without getting caught. He'd get the flashlight while he was at it.

Ears on high alert, he tiptoed along. Dishes clanked in the kitchen sink. The murmur of his parents' voices rose and fell.

Not far now.

The living room cabinet came into view. His bare feet moved silently across the carpet.

In a few hours, if all went according to plan, he'd be running across a different carpet in the Winchester House. The one Dad had installed in a room called the

Witches Cap. That carpet was a strange shade of blue —*haint-blue,* that's what Dad called it. Even the name sounded funny. Supposedly the *haint-blue* color fooled the spirits because it looked like water and spirits were scared of water.

Or so people said.

Anyway, forget *haint-blue,* who called a room the *Witches Cap?*

He couldn't wait to see it. And get a picture of it. Especially because that's where Pete was headed last year when he'd tried to sneak inside. Double win!

A floorboard creaked.

"What do you think you're doing?" Dad's voice boomed. "What part of staying in your room don't you understand?"

Jesse jumped. Whoa. Way to look guilty.

"Just looking for a snack," he said.

"Back to your room. You already had dinner."

The telephone rang. Saved by the bell!

Dad went to answer it.

Heart slamming, Jesse darted to the cabinet and grabbed the flashlight and camera.

Crash.

Oh no!

He'd knocked over a framed family picture—a skinny Pete, seven years old, struggling to hold a chubby toddler. Jesse. Both were laughing. Both were hanging onto each other, their brown eyes so alike. When had things changed?

They didn't laugh together much now.

Quietly, Jesse set the picture back on the sideboard. Then he sprinted to his room and locked the door.

CHAPTER 5

At a quarter to eleven, Jesse pulled on a dark-blue shirt and loaded up his knapsack with the flashlight and Kodak Brownie. Then, he slid open his bedroom window.

Creeeeeeeak.

He winced and listened for Dad's footsteps.

Silence.

Quietly, he swung his legs over the sill and scrambled onto the flat roof.

"Come on, Sniffer," he whispered.

Sniffer followed, his ears quivering.

They crossed carefully to the garage roof, dropped onto a pile of wooden planking supplies, and then onto the grass.

Sniffer galloped around, racing up and down the lawn. He thought this was some new game. At any moment, the lab would bark, and it would be all over.

"Shh, down boy. Good dog!" Jesse grabbed Sniffer's leather collar and hurried away from the farmstead.

An eerie quiet filled the country lane. In the distance, across dry, lumpy fields and leafless orchards, the Winchester House loomed against the sky.

Jesse broke into a jog with Sniffer trotting at his side.

Overhead, clouds, like dark sky-dragons, flew across the bright half-moon.

Something caught his eye. Black shapes, hundreds of them.

What the . . .

Birds, the sky teemed with them!

How weird. Birds didn't fly at night, not as far as he knew. But there they were, flocks of geese, wings flapping. Some soared high above, some barely missed his head as they swooped past.

Freaked out, he ducked.

Now, a flock of pigeons flew by, right at eye level. He dodged, throwing up his arms. Where were they going? Did they know something he didn't? Maybe they were running from the coming storm?

In that case, he'd better get a move on.

He'd barely started running when his feet slid on something wet and mushy. Catching his balance, he saw the road was crawling with earthworms. Ugh! They squished under his sneakers.

A group of rabbits hopped by.

Sniffer lunged.

"No! No chasing rabbits." Jesse pulled Sniffer back.

In the distance, coyotes howled. Long, echoing howls. Hairs rose on Jesse's neck. Something was off. Why were the birds on the move? And the rabbits? Even the worms?

Well, he had other things to worry about. He needed to get inside the house before it started pouring and drenched Dad's precious camera.

As if on cue, thunder rumbled. He ran.

Emma, wearing a navy dress, black stockings, and boots, stood waiting for him at the Winchester House gate.

"You came!" he called, grinning.

"Yep. We have to show up your brother once in a while, right?" Her frizzy blond hair was tied with green ribbons.

A kid stepped out from behind her back, small and skinny and dressed in a sailor suit with a floppy blue cap over his long, white-blond hair.

The shrimp started doing his best to kick down the wrought-iron gate.

Jesse stifled a groan, inched up to Emma, and whispered, "Why'd you bring GL?"

"I had to," Emma said. "I'm babysitting him."

"I thought it was your sister's turn."

"He kicked her. So, she dumped him on me. I couldn't just leave him."

George, or GL—short for Greased Lightning—was a four-year-old terror.

Jesse scratched at his hair, turning it into spikes. "Yeah, but . . . we can't take him inside," he said as GL started body-slamming the gates. "You know what he's like!"

Emma crossed her arms. "You wanted me to come, I'm here."

GL abandoned the gate and hollered, "Hey Jesse! Make Sniffer do the trick. Make him do it!"

Emma rolled her green eyes. "He got into the candy. He's completely bonkers. Worse than usual."

"Make him do it!" GL shouted.

Jesse pulled his black baseball cap lower. "Sniffer will do his trick later. Promise. We have to stay quiet."

"Now!" GL shouted. "Now! Do it now!"

Sniffer's tail was down. He slunk behind Jesse. Maybe all the geese and weird animals were creeping him out. Plus, he didn't like thunder.

Jesse stroked the lab's soft dark fur. "Sniffer doesn't want to right now."

"Make him do his trick!" GL yelled.

"Shh!" Jesse said. "You can't come if you keep yelling like a baby."

"Make him do his trick," GL whispered. "Please, please, puh-lease."

"Just do it," Emma said, glancing at the road. "Someone's going to see us. If my parents find out I took GL, I'm dead."

Jesse said, "Give me one of your sneakers, GL. Quick."

GL pulled off a sneaker and handed it over.

"Hide behind that plum tree down there," Jesse said.

"Don't let Sniffer see where I go," GL said.

"I won't. I'm turning him around."

Beaming a gap-toothed smile, GL ran off along the lane.

Jesse held the sneaker under Sniffer's nose. "This shouldn't take long. Pee-ew, this sneaker stinks just like GL."

Sniffer stuck his nose into the sneaker.

"Got it? Good dog! Seek. Seek GL!"

Sniffer sniffed the air and the road with his big, wet nose, doing his super-scent-tracker thing. Within seconds, he made a beeline for the plum tree where GL was hiding.

GL ran back, giggling with delight. "Good dog, Sniffer!"

Emma beamed. "How did you train him to do that? It's amazing."

"Dogs can smell forty times better than humans," Jesse said, knowing Emma loved her facts.

"Ooh, that's neat. Forty times?"

"Yeah, but can you imagine? That means stinky stuff is forty times stinkier."

They both laughed at that.

GL yelled, "Super stinky!"

Jesse put his finger to his lips. "Come on, let's do this. Follow me."

The iron gate was fastened with a thick chain and padlock. Checking that no one was watching, Jesse slid through a narrow gap between the gate and the fence, and the others followed.

CHAPTER 6

Winchester House
11:05 PM.

Jesse, Emma, and GL stood in a row, all staring up at the spooky Winchester House. It loomed over them, monstrous in the moonlight.

A lightning bolt highlighted the endless towers, turrets, and cupolas, while the dark, dark windows reflected like eyes.

Hold on, something moved in one of the windows! But the place was supposed to be empty. Jesse squinted, trying to catch sight of it again.

Wind rustled the trees. A weathervane on the top of a cupola moved. But in the window, all was still.

"What's up?" Emma asked.

"I thought I saw someone watching from up there."

24

Emma frowned. "A caretaker?"

"I probably imagined it."

"I don't want to go in there if there's some massive Frankenstein caretaker inside."

"Who said massive? Anyway, no one's there."

GL said, "Bats in the belfry!"

Emma rolled her eyes. "Where did you hear that expression?"

"Ghosts," GL replied, as if that made sense.

Jesse took a deep breath. "There are no ghosts."

"Are you sure about that?" Emma asked

"I don't know." He raised his camera. "Can you imagine if I got a picture of one, though? They'd print it in every paper in America."

"Haha." Emma laughed nervously. "Don't tell me that's why we're here. I thought you wanted to get pictures of the weird stairs and stuff."

Lightning flashed again. High above, the pointy Bell Tower stood out in sharp relief.

Emma pointed at it. "I wonder why Mrs. Winchester rings the bell every midnight."

Jesse started to reply but held his tongue. Better not to mention that—according to Dad—she rang it to summon the angry spirits. She'd have some kind of meeting with them to announce her building plans. Then she'd ring it again at two in the morning to send them away.

What a strange way to live.

Well, as long as they didn't ring the bell, the spirits wouldn't show up.

Except, what if he summoned them? And got a picture of it?

While terrifying, that would be something.

He shivered. Did he dare? Did he even want to see a ghost? In a way, he did because Pete would go nuts with jealousy, and Jesse could tell all the guys at school about it.

Emma probably wouldn't like it, though.

And what if Sarah Winchester was right, that the spirits were after revenge? Jesse had shot a Winchester rifle lots of time, even if he'd never taken down a bird. Dad worked on this house. And Gramps helped design the gun. Would the spirits come after him if he snuck inside? Would they attack him?

He shivered again. He wasn't sure if the shiver was excitement or fear. "Let's go before it gets too late and someone finds us gone."

A paved path wound past a fountain and around a

rose garden. A sickly-sweet smell of rotting rose petals filled the air.

"Look at all these varieties," Emma said, naming off roses as they went. Sometimes she sounded like a walking encyclopedia.

They neared the front porch. Up close, the monster-sized mansion looked like some kid built it using weirded-out giant blocks.

GL squeaked and skidded to a stop. Jesse almost fell right over him.

"G-g-ghost!" GL stammered.

Jesse gulped. A white figure hovered at the massive front door. Spirits already! He froze and realized what it was.

"Statue," he said. "That's just a statue."

"Duh." GL stuck out his tongue and crossed his eyes. "I knew it."

"Did not," Jesse said.

"*You* didn't." GL giggled. "You peed your pants."

Jesse rolled his eyes. "Right, as if!" A few drops of rain spattered his face. "Let's go round the back and find a basement window," he said. "Basement windows are easiest to get through."

Emma said, "Stay close, GL, don't go running off."

Jesse helped GL through a narrow space between a brick tower and the main wall of the House. Emma and Sniffer followed.

Wind howled across the courtyard. Leafless branches clawed the sky, skeletal in the dark.

Crack!

He jumped. What was that?

Emma grabbed his arm. "Sounded like a gunshot." Wind whipped her hair. "Someone's shooting at us!" She dropped to her stomach, pulling GL down. "Hit the ground!

Jesse crouched low. "Must be a hunter out in the fields."

Another crack. Louder than the first.

"A hunter? Not in the middle of the night," Emma said.

"Er . . . maybe not."

It sure sounded like gunshots. Dad said there were rifles in a display cabinet in the House. Could the spirits have got hold of them? Were the spirits shooting at them?

A gruesome thought arose: *Maybe they want to take over our warm, living bodies.* No—that was aliens, not ghosts. Ghosts didn't take over human bodies, did they? Or maybe they did.

Gramps once told him, *You have nothing to fear, except fear itself—if you don't mind the consequences.*

Trouble was, he hadn't worked out what that meant.

Gramps often talked in riddles and gave dire warnings. And Gramps had been around so long that he saw danger everywhere. Probably, rightly so. Maybe danger did lurk everywhere. But a kid had to take risks once in a while, or life would be totally boring!

Squinting, he scanned the back courtyard. Empty.

Another gust of cold wind.

Another loud crack.

A branch hit the ground, barely missing GL's head.

Jesse blew out a relieved laugh. "It's dead tree branches. The wind is breaking them."

"Oh, of course!" Emma said. "They're all extra dry because of the drought. Good thing this rain is coming. We need it."

"Come on, let's find that basement window."

A fat raindrop hit Jesse's nose.

"Here it comes," Emma said. "Get under the eaves. We can track along the back wall until we find a way in."

"Good idea."

Moments later, Jesse pulled aside the branches of a fig tree and saw a narrow basement window. "Jackpot!"

The shutters opened with a push.

Easy. Too easy.

Jesse frowned. It looked like someone had climbed through here recently. Were squatters living inside? If so, he didn't want to run into them.

He wiped the thought away, squeezed inside, and dropped to the floor.

Turning, he held out his arms, "GL, you're next."

After GL, they got Sniffer safely through.

Last came Emma.

The whole group was inside. They'd done it. They were here.

CHAPTER 7

WINCHESTER HOUSE
THE BASEMENT

Jesse, Emma, GL, and Sniffer stood for a long moment, frozen in silence. Jesse listened for squatters but heard nothing.

A breeze whispered, and creepy fingers brushed his face.

He reeled back.

Sniffer barked.

Only cobwebs. Get a grip!

He blinked hard, waiting for his eyes to adjust. They didn't. This place was darker than dark. Nothing was creepier than a pitch-dark basement. Except, maybe, a basement with a basement squatter. Or a spirit. Yeah, a basement with a spirit or two would be horrible. Anything could be hiding in the corners. Or under the stairs.

"Dark," GL whispered. "Dark, dark, dark!"

"Hold on," Jesse said. He dug into his pocket for the flashlight and worked to find the button. Suddenly, light blazed.

"Whoa!" Emma said. "Where did you get that?"

"Borrowed it from my dad," Jesse said. "But he doesn't know. It's a flashlight." He panned it around the room, sending light bouncing and casting shadows everywhere.

Hulking dark shapes loomed. Just furniture, he told himself. Sheet-covered furniture. Trunks and boxes, and old stuff nobody wanted. What a huge basement, filled with hidey-holes—hordes of squatters could be living down here. Yikes! The House was every bit as spooky as he'd thought it would be. Maybe even too spooky. It smelled bad—dank and musty. Like something died. Maybe the last squatter. But probably a rat.

Emma sneezed. "The dust is tickling my nose."

"Me too," GL whined. His little button nose twitched. "I want to go home."

"Let's just look around for a few minutes." Jesse placed the Kodak Brownie on a box to keep it steady, opened the shutter, and pressed the side lever. He heard the click.

"It's too dark to get a good picture," Emma said.

"I know. But maybe I'll get something. Let's go." Jesse led the way up a creaking, long stairway, only to find that it looped sideways and started going down again instead of rising to the first floor.

Jesse stood scratching his head. Without warning, GL climbed onto the wooden banister. He slid away, yelling at the top of his lungs.

There was a pause and then a wail, "I'm back in the basement! I hate the basement!"

"Well, you better get back up here," Emma yelled.

"Crazy!" Jesse grinned. "Why build a staircase that comes halfway up from the basement and goes straight down again?" He aimed the flashlight at the stairs and took another picture. His friends at school would love this weird stairway.

"Imagine building it," Emma said. "It's enough to make your head go funny."

"Maybe that's what happened to my dad. He's been super uptight since he started working here."

They waited for GL and then tramped along the strange stairs until they spotted a landing. If you climbed over the banister, you could just reach the landing.

One by one, they clambered onto it, then walked forward to see patterned windows. Moonlight filtered inside. A maze of corridors led deeper into the house to their left and right.

"What do you think, which way?" Jesse said.

"Well, if we always turn right, we can do the opposite to find our way back," Emma said.

"Smart. Except look at that corridor. It has no doors and ends at a blank wall. It's the corridor to nowhere."

Instead of laughing, Emma shivered, wrapping her arms around herself. "I wouldn't want to be lost in here."

"Check out the portraits!" The beam from Jesse's flashlight bobbed over life-sized portraits of solemn men and women.

Emma said, "Those are some fancy clothes, all velvet and satin. Look at the jewels! Emeralds. Diamonds."

"The Winchesters sure were rich," Jesse said.

"Yes, but unlucky. Sarah Winchester's husband died young. And her daughter had some strange problem and died, too."

Out of the corner of Jesse's eye, he saw something move. Whipping around, he came face-to-face with a portrait of a regal-looking woman in coronet-like braids. She stared back at him, thin lips turned down, eyes grave and disapproving.

As he began to turn away, her gaze followed.

Yikes. Did her eyes really move?

He stared at her again. Inscrutable, she stared back.

Huh. Must have been the flashlight. Don't be nuts.

"Let's get going, I'm getting the creeps," Emma said.

GL was strangely silent as they crept along.

Emma whispered, "I don't know if staying-on-the-right is working. Didn't we walk this way already?"

"I'm not sure." Jesse felt lost but didn't want to say so out loud. The House seemed designed to make you lose your way.

They crept up a steep stairway with teeny-tiny steps.

"My shoes hardly fit on these stairs," Jesse said, walking on tiptoe.

Emma said, "Imagine living in here? What if you had to go to the bathroom or wanted to get a snack from the kitchen?"

"Or answer the telephone," Jesse said.

"Imagine getting lost in your own house!" Emma said. *Bang.*

His head hit the ceiling.

GL giggled, the first noise he'd made in ages. "Funny!"

"Whoa!" Rubbing his head, he looked up. "That is kind of funny. I banged my head. This staircase goes nowhere!"

Emma gave a surprised laugh. "That's so strange! Why build it?"

"I guess to fool the spirits," Jesse said.

Emma glanced around. "Spirits aren't real. But if they are, I don't want to see any. We should go."

"Soon. Let's just look around a little longer."

"Building this place must cost oodles," Emma whispered as they clambered back down and paused on a landing furnished with velvet sofas and chairs.

"Gramps says the Winchesters made a fortune like you'd never believe off those rifles," Jesse said.

"Like how much?"

"I don't know. Enough to build a million crazy rooms. Dad and his carpenters come here almost every day to build more. Extensions everywhere."

Emma said. "If I had that much money, I'd build a big game room and put a pool table in it, and we could be pool sharks!"

"I want to play sharks!" GL said. "I like swimming pools."

Jesse grinned. "Different kind of pool."

"Has your dad seen any ghosts?" Emma asked.

"No," Jesse said. "But he never comes inside the house at night."

An icy gust swept down the hallway.

Emma whirled around. "Did you feel that?"

Jesse shrugged. "Just the wind."

"What wind?" Emma said. "The windows are closed."

Bang! A door slammed shut.

Emma grabbed Jesse's arm in a crushing grip. "What made that door slam?"

"I want to go home," GL whined.

Emma said, "He's right, we should go. We did it, we got in here, now come on. Let's leave."

"What about the Witches Cap? Don't you want to see it?"

Emma shoved her hands into her frizzy hair and stared at the ceiling.

Jesse said, "Just one picture."

She groaned. Her face looked pale in the flashlight's

glow. "Why is it called the Witches Cap? Are there supposed to be witches in here, too?"

"No. It's just a name."

The name of the place that the spirits supposedly come after Sarah Winchester rings the bells at midnight. But it wasn't midnight.

"What are you hiding, Jesse?" Emma said.

"I'm just thinking we should get there before . . . before the bell rings. You know?"

"Who's going to ring the bell if Sarah Winchester isn't home?"

"Excellent point."

"Let's get this over with," Emma said, marching off with GL and Sniffer in tow.

Even though Emma was stomping along, he realized that—scared or not—she'd never miss out on seeing the Witches Cap. Not if he was going there. They pretty much did everything together, even if they didn't always agree on things.

Jesse felt buzzed. There might even be wispy spirits hovering inside. He'd be careful; he'd keep his distance. But if he captured them on film, he'd be famous.

He put his eye up to the Kodak Brownie's viewer, opened the shutter, and took another picture of the stairway. He wished cameras came equipped with lights. He'd never get a good shot in these dark rooms.

At least the moon was shining through the racing clouds. He needed to find a room with big windows letting in more moonlight.

"I'm thirsty," GL said.

"That's because you ate too much candy," Emma said.

"You're being mean," GL yelled. "I'm going to tell my mommy on you."

"Well, you *did* eat too much candy," Emma said.

"I'm going to tell my mommy you brought me here and were mean to me," GL wailed.

The noise was way too loud, making Jesse cringe and glance around.

"Oh great," Emma said. "Now GL's going to blab."

Jesse glared at GL. "Snitches get stitches and end up in ditches."

Right away, seeing GL's scared face, Jesse wished he could take it back. Snitch or not, GL looked terrified, and he was only four. Jesse recalled how Pete said mean things to him. He didn't want to be like that.

"No!" GL wailed, crossing his legs and grabbing his pants. "I need to go potty."

Jesse said, "Uh oh."

"What?" Emma said.

"Dad says there's only one working toilet. And I have no idea how to find it."

CHAPTER 8

Jesse went to GL and said, "Don't worry, buddy, we'll figure this out." But he wasn't sure how.

Standing in the shadowy hallway, GL wailed, "I need to go potty! I need to go potty!"

Emma said, "Hundreds of rooms and only one working toilet? What a nightmare! Why?"

"The rest are fake to fool the spirits."

"Spirits need to use the toilet?" Emma said.

"All I know is that there's only one that works, and I have no clue where it is."

Emma shot GL a worried glance.

"I need to go. NOW." GL jumped up and down.

"Okay. Just hold it. We'll find the toilet." Jesse led the way back along the hallway. A steep stairway went down to a landing, and a spiraling stairway rose to a level two stories above. No toilet. He turned around.

"We can try upstairs," he said. "Maybe that's where the bedrooms and bathrooms are. The toilet must be up there."

Jesse led the way up the long, spiraling stairway. Double doors opened to a cavernous Grand Ballroom covered with carved woodwork right up to the twelve-foot-high ceiling. A gold and silver chandelier swung slowly.

Moonlight shone through stained-glass windows, highlighting the silver spiderweb patterns. That could make an interesting picture. He grabbed the Kodak Brownie from his knapsack.

"Look! There's writing on those windows over there." Emma read slowly. "*Wide un-clasp the tables of their thoughts. These same thoughts people this little world.* That's a quote from Shakespeare."

"Is it?" The odd words made Jesse uneasy. This was a serious, dark place with a strange feel. "Do you think the quote is about spirits?"

Emma looked thoughtful. "I think it's two quotes

from different Shakespeare plays. Maybe Sarah Winchester wanted it to be about spirits."

Sudden gloomy music filled the room.

Jesse whirled around.

GL was thumping the keys of a big pump organ.

"Hey! Stop that!" Jesse said.

"You can't make me." GL climbed up onto the organ and stood defiant, thumping the keys with his feet.

"Get off there," Jesse said. "You'll break it!"

With one final bang, GL climbed down and began jumping back and forth on the dark and light parquet squares. "I need to go potty!"

Sniffer growled. A low warning growl in the back of his throat.

Jesse started and nearly dropped the flashlight. A ghostly white fog swirled in the far-left corner of the Ballroom. A figure was materializing. Whoa! The figure was long and thin, with hair like squiggly octopus tentacles.

"There's something over there," Jesse whispered.

Emma jumped behind Jesse and peered over his shoulder. "What sort of thing?"

"A weird thing. Look!" Jesse pointed. "Might be a spirit. I've got to get a picture."

Emma clutched his arm. "Okay. But fast. Then let's get out."

Jesse set the Kodak Brownie on a table to steady the shot and opened the shutter.

"Hurry!" Emma hissed. "It moved!"

With a sudden shriek, GL charged out of the Ballroom.

Emma made a futile grab for her nephew. "GL! Hey! Get back here!"

Jesse raced after GL.

The kid was already at the far end of the corridor, scrambling up a steep, narrow stairway.

"Get back here!" Jesse yelled. He started up the stairway, with Emma and Sniffer right behind him.

At the top of the stairs, GL scrambled like a crab onto a landing. Jesse grabbed his ankle. GL's floppy blue hat flew over the wooden banister and down into the pool of darkness below.

"My hat!" GL yelled.

"I hear footsteps," Emma said. "We've got to hide."

Jesse could hear footsteps too. Shuffling footsteps, coming up the stairs. Eyes bugging, he searched for an escape. All five doors facing the landing were closed. He grabbed the closest doorknob.

"Locked," he gulped.

They tried more, but all were locked.

Jesse tried another. As he held on, the brass knob rattled and began to turn of its own accord.

Yikes!

Sniffer barked.

"Someone's t-t-turning it from the other side," Emma stammered. "Don't let them out!"

Hands shaking, Jesse clung to the doorknob. It wasn't working! How long could he keep holding it?

"I'm going to count. When I get to three, we run," he whispered. "We dive through the first open door we find and lock ourselves in."

Emma nodded and grabbed GL's hand.

"I have to go potty," GL whimpered.

"One, two, three," Jesse hissed.

Panting, they raced down a wood-paneled corridor and dived into the first open room. It was a bedroom, a very grand bedroom, with a big, four-poster bed. Long red velvet drapes framed daisy-patterned windows. Moonlight cast blue shadows everywhere.

Jesse tried to lock the door.

The keyhole was empty. He needed the key to turn the bolt!

"Find the key," he hissed. "Quick!"

Frantic, flashlight in hand, Emma pulled open the desk drawers and shuffled through the papers inside.

GL ran into a bathroom.

"See if there's a key in there," Jesse called.

"Toilet!" GL cried in delight.

Jesse was hot with fear. Surely there was a key somewhere.

From down the corridor, he heard a banging sound.

Emma cried out. "They're coming."

Someone or something was coming down the hallway, banging on doors.

Bang!

Bang!

Bang!

"W-w-what's that?" Emma stammered.

"It's not good," Jesse replied as the room grew icy cold.

"Could be the wind," said Emma in a hopeful, trembling voice.

"Dad says the house has two thousand doors." Why

Jesse said it, he had no idea.

"Two thousand?" Emma said. "What does that matter now? Look at Sniffer! He's petrified."

Sniffer lay on his back, his legs in the air.

"Dogs can sense spirits," she added. "I read it in a book."

"We don't know that for certain." Jesse crouched, putting his arm around the dog.

GL lurched out of the bathroom. "It's coming to get us! It's coming!"

It was. The banging grew nearer and nearer.

The room was tombstone cold.

Something, someone, thumped on their door.

Jesse jumped. The banging went right through his body. Emma joined him, and they put their backs against the door, leaning on it to keep it shut.

Whatever this thing was, it was nuts.

And menacing.

Real menacing.

"Maybe it's the cops!" Emma whispered. "Maybe someone saw us and reported us."

"I wish," Jesse said. He'd love to see two policemen right now. But they would have said they were police.

The door shook. Cripes!

"Maybe it will go to another room," Emma whispered.

Crash!

"It's trying to break the door down," Jesse whispered.

Jesse shot a look at GL. The kid stood silhouetted in the bathroom door. He'd gone strangely silent and wore a weird, blank stare.

The banging ratcheted up to a fever pitch. The noise was deafening. Sometimes it sounded as if it was in the room next door. Then in the room across the hall. Then it was at their door again.

"What is it?" Emma whispered. "What does it think it's doing? Is it banging with its whole body? Does it have a body?"

The hammering on their door switched to little patting sounds. Like something was feeling around the edges, looking for a way in.

The patting sounds were almost worse than the banging.

Jesse threw himself away from the door and grabbed the oak dresser. "Help me pull this. We need to block the way in!"

Together, he and Emma dragged it into place. Would it keep out whatever was trying to get in?

Bang!

Bang!

"Go away," Jesse shouted. "You can't get in."

For a moment, there was dead silence.

Then the banging returned.

"Great," Emma groaned. "Now it knows for sure that we're in here."

Pounding—furious pounding shook the whole room. The handle rattled furiously as if something meant to open it no matter what.

CHAPTER 9

WINCHESTER HOUSE
THE DAISY BEDROOM

Jesse glanced at Emma and suddenly felt horrible for bringing her, GL, and Sniffer here.

Whatever was chasing him, he hated it. This was exactly how he felt when Pete had him in a headlock because he was bigger and knew how to get away with it.

They added more furniture to the dresser blocking the doorway—a heavy armchair, side tables, a wooden trunk.

He climbed atop it all and thumped on the door himself, hard. "Leave us alone! We didn't do anything to you. Leave us alone, or you'll be sorry!"

Emma stared, horrified. "Cool it, Jesse! I don't think you should threaten it."

"Listen," GL squeaked. "It's talking."

Talking? More like hissing. The eerie sounds swirled

46

through the keyhole. Words began to form, words that made Jesse's stomach clench.

Help me, Jesse, help me.

Emma cried, "It knows your name. How does it know your name?"

"I . . . I don't know."

"Wait, is this a trick?" Emma said in a shaky voice. She crossed her arms; the flashlight beam danced across the wall. "Are you tricking us? You better tell me right now."

"No! Why would I do that?" Jesse said.

"To scare us."

"We're best friends, Emma," Jesse said. "I'd never trick you."

Emma shot him a skeptical look.

"I mean it." His lips felt chapped, his tongue dry. "I don't know what's going on. But I'll get us out of here. I promise."

How he had no idea. Usually, Emma was the brainy one who got them out of scrapes. But she was glaring at him like this was up to him now.

Maybe they imagined the voice. Maybe they'd been watching too many horror movies. In the movie theater, it was fun joining the audience as they shouted: *Don't go in there!*

But this wasn't fun. Not in real life.

Through the daisy-patterned windows, moonlight shone on GL's white-blond hair. Racing clouds cast ghoulish shadows. The air smelled of mothballs and fear.

He was about to say, *Let's go, I'll open the door, and we'll run,* when the voice hissed again.

Jesse . . . Jesse! Come out, come out wherever you are!

Standing next to Jesse, GL yanked on his sleeve. "It wants you."

Emma groaned. "We'll never get past it. That thing is waiting for us to open the door."

An awful realization struck. Of course, the spirits wanted Jesse. His very own gramps had helped build the famous Winchester repeating rifle. The spirit must know! It was thirsting for revenge!

And he'd brought his best friend, his dog, and GL into this mess.

Emma gripped his arm.

"Maybe if we stay in here long enough, it will leave," he said, turning to her.

Except Emma wasn't holding onto him at all. She wasn't even close. Emma was crouched way over behind the writing table with her arms around GL.

Frantic, Jesse squinted around the bedroom, searching for another door. "There's got to be another way out. Hand me the flashlight."

"No," GL said. "It wants you to stay."

"Quit it," Jesse said. "Don't say that."

"Yes. Quit it," Emma said.

GL gave a strange, maniacal grin. His little white teeth shone in the dark. "Snitches get stitches."

Jesse had never noticed GL's sharp, little incisors. Or what pale-blue eyes GL had. Lightning flashed outside, and GL's eyes seemed to glow.

"It wants you to stay," GL said in almost a man's voice. "Jesse, *JESSE!*"

"Stop that right now," Emma said, yanking him to face her. "Stop it."

GL leaped forward and sank his teeth into Emma's arm.

Emma shrieked.

With a gasp, Jesse grabbed the kid and yanked him off.

GL snarled.

Emma rubbed her arm. "You hurt me. Look! You drew blood. Why'd you do that, GL?"

"Snitches get stitches and end up in ditches." GL laughed wildly.

"What's the matter with you?" Jesse said.

Had an evil spirit taken over the poor kid? Cripes, what would GL's mother say if they took him home like this? The kid stood frozen, staring into space.

"We have to get out of here," Emma said. "He's gone crazy. Maybe he needs a doctor."

Jesse pulled up GL's eyelids, suspicious. "Maybe he's faking it?"

"We need to get him home."

There was a distant sound of cackling laughter.

Sniffer crawled under the bed.

Jesse felt panic rise. Sniffer was usually a great guard dog. He loved barking at anything threatening.

Cackling laughter swirled, echoing, bouncing. He gripped his head with both hands. It wasn't coming from the hallway. Was someone hiding in the bedroom?

"Enough!" he shouted and ran around, pulling back the long, red drapes. "Show yourself! Come out!"

Another cackle.

It was coming from the bathroom.

Emma handed him the flashlight and watched as he approached the bathroom's partially open door. Inside, thirteen narrow windows lined the wall. Each window held thirteen panels of glass.

A gurgle rose from the shower stall drain. It sounded like a shower monster itching to get out. Was that where the laughter came from?

No, impossible.

He shone the beam on the wood-paneled wall above the sink. It held thirteen round holes.

He peered into one. And whipped back as a hiss came through.

This was it! Whoa!

Wait, was this some sort of communication panel? So that people in different rooms could talk to one another? Yes, the holes were labeled, with the names of other rooms.

"Emma. Get in here. Listen to this,' he whispered. "The weird voice is coming from this hole. These are communication holes. They're marked to show which room they come from."

She inched up to him with a now silent GL in tow. "If that's true, and I believe you're right, which room is the noise coming from?"

Jesse leaned in to read the writing. "The Witches Cap."

The place where the midnight meeting of spirits took place. But no one had rung the bell. Had the spirits come anyway out of habit?

Emma pressed her ear to the hole. She leaped away as if it was burning hot. "Someone's there! I heard them talking. There's someone in the house."

CHAPTER 10

WINCHESTER HOUSE
THE DAISY BEDROOM

The bells in the Bell Tower began to peal.

"Someone's up there ringing those," Emma whispered. "Bells can't ring themselves."

Bong . . . bong . . . bong . . .

On and on they rang. Twelve chimes in total.

"It's midnight," Jesse whispered.

The Witching Hour.

Jesse said, "Um—I probably should have told you this before, but—"

"Told me what?"

He gulped. "Sarah Winchester rings the bells at midnight to call the spirits."

"Wait, she does *what*?" Emma whisper-shouted. "And you're only telling me this now?"

"She's not here, I figured the bells wouldn't ring, there would be no summoning."

Emma grabbed her mass of frizzy hair. "Why would she even want to summon a bunch of spirits?"

"Dad said she talks to them about the house. She uses this thing called a Ouija board."

"That's just creepy. I saw a Ouija board once, Mother wouldn't even let me touch it. It looked like a game board decorated with the alphabet, and it had a pointy arrow thing. You put your finger on the arrow and ask a question. The spirits make the arrow move, and they spell out an answer."

But Jesse was still thinking about the bells. "Sarah Winchester must have come home early. Or maybe she never left at all."

"How can she live in an awful place like this? Maybe she knows we're here. Maybe she's the one who's been making all that noise. To scare us."

"Maybe, but I know one thing."

Emma shot him a sideways glance. "Oh yeah?"

"I'm not leaving without a picture of her using that Ouija board in the Witches Cap."

She glared at him. "Forget it, Jesse, I'm done. I came here, I'm scared out of my mind, and we're leaving."

The house had gone oddly silent. It was like it was listening.

Jesse breathed out. "Look, you take the flashlight. I'll meet you guys outside. I've just got to get a picture! Otherwise, why did I even come here?"

Emma looked skyward with a frustrated noise.

"This is important," Jesse said.

"Fine. But I'm definitely leaving. Look at GL! I need to get him away from this place."

Jesse snapped his fingers in front of GL's glassy eyes.

GL just stared.

Maybe he was in shock?

"Yeah," Jesse admitted. "You better get him home."

"Wait, how am I supposed to do that?" She pointed at the furniture they'd piled in front of the door. "Even if I could get out, I don't exactly want to meet whatever's in that hallway."

Jesse glanced around thoughtfully. "I'm pretty sure this house is loaded with secret passageways. Maybe there's another way out?"

Emma didn't bother to reply. Instead, she started running her hands over the walls. Jesse did the same. After checking the whole room, he gave up. If there were fake panels, he couldn't find them.

"Look under the carpets," he said. "Maybe there's a trap door."

Emma rolled up the Persian rug. "Nothing."

Jesse pulled open the closet. "Jackpot," he called.

Yes! In front of him, a dark, narrow passage led to a steep, rising stairwell. Emma was beside him in an instant, tugging GL along.

"But it goes up," Emma said. "We want to go down."

"You know the stairs in this place, they go all sorts of ways. Maybe this one goes up and then down on the other side."

Emma went first, dragging GL. Glad to have Sniffer by his side, Jesse grabbed his dog collar to help him up the narrow stairs. It ended at a funny, waist-high door.

Emma whispered, "I hear voices."

Jesse put his ear against the tiny door and listened. Voices came to him, low and muffled.

Emma backed away. "We better turn around."

Jesse said, "We don't know for sure that's where the voices are coming from. This is our best way out."

Slowly, he cracked open the small door. It was so low he had to stoop to see through.

The room that stretched before him seemed like a place spirits would love—huge, gloomy, and octagonal, with a high domed ceiling that looked perfect for floating in the air.

As for the carpet, he shivered. It was a watery shade of blue.

Haint-blue.

Which could only mean . . .

A thrill of terror and excitement rushed through him. "The Witches Cap," he whispered.

Emma muttered, "Oh no."

Sniffer gave a low growl.

Jesse crept forward, peering into the gloom.

Red, purple, and yellow satin cloaks hung on hooks to his right. He counted quickly. Thirteen cloaks. Thirteen hooks. Lots of things in the house seemed to come in thirteens, from the windowpanes to the wooden panels.

He'd always thought thirteen was an unlucky number.

But maybe tonight, he'd be lucky. Maybe he'd get a picture for the newspaper. Maybe they'd escape without being caught. Maybe this would be their best adventure ever, one they'd talk about for the rest of their lives.

Or maybe the opposite. That was too awful to consider.

As his eyes adjusted to the layered dark, he spied three tall, shadowy figures in the room's distant corner. He froze, but none turned around. So far, Jesse hadn't been spotted.

An oil lamp hung from the ceiling, lighting the top of their heads. The high collars of black capes hid their faces. Jesse squinted, trying to see better.

Who were they? It couldn't be Sarah Winchester, Dad said she was only around four feet tall. Cripes, who were they?

"They look like the Salem witches," Emma whispered.

Jesse put his finger to his lips. What if this was a real live witches' coven?

The figures seated themselves at the round table.

Behind him, he heard Emma's nervous breathing. He could feel GL's head wedged against the back of his knees. If either made a noise, the witches would hear for sure.

Spellbound, he watched the witchlike figures place their fingers on a wooden board.

"Ouija board," Emma whispered.

"Shh!"

He blinked to see better. What a time to be nearsighted. Was this a séance? Were they calling up spirits?

A deep voice made him jump.

"Who are you?" the voice boomed.

CHAPTER 11

WINCHESTER HOUSE
THE WITCHES CAP

"Who are you?" the voice boomed again.

Oh no. The witches had seen him! Jesse nearly stammered out a reply.

Then he realized the question was addressed to the spirits.

The arrow moved slowly across the Ouija board in the cloaked figures' hands. It paused now and then, probably stopping at the letters. The spirits were spelling out a message. An excited murmur passed between the three witches.

Emma nudged Jesse and pointed to an open, arched door. She raised her eyebrows in a question.

Jesse nodded. Could work. They had to try. While the

witches concentrated on the Ouija board, he, Emma, and GL could tiptoe across the room.

He raised one finger, motioning her to hold on a second.

Hands shaking, he steadied the Kodak Brownie on his knee and opened the shutter so light could pass through the lens. It was a long shot but the best he could do. He squinted through the mirrored viewfinder and pressed the side lever.

JESSE'S KODAK BROWNIE CAMERA

The Ouija arrow kept moving. One of the witches began to read out letters:

A—V—I—C—T—I—M

A second hissed, "*A victim!*"

"Why have you come to us?" boomed the deep voice.

"W-a-i-t-i-n-g," came the hissed reply. "It says it's waiting."

"Waiting for what?"

"F-o-r-j-e-s-s-e."

Waiting for Jesse.

Emma gasped, and Jesse's heart lurched. It *did* know Jesse's name. It knew he was here!

Gulping for air, he snapped a picture. If he was going to die, maybe someone would find the film and know what happened.

Without warning, GL shoved past and bolted across the room. With a desperate look at Jesse, Emma flew after him. They disappeared through the arched door.

Jesse took another picture wildly.

Time to get out of Dodge. One witch, a tall figure with white, luminous skin, glided across the Witches Cap, claw-like hands reaching for him.

Fast as a greyhound, Jesse streaked across the Witches Cap, out the arched door, and slid down a hallway.

Sniffer was glued to his side, nails clicking on the wooden floor.

Mirrors lined the corridor. Jesse saw four reflections of himself, googly-eyed with fear, and four Sniffers. When he skidded around a corner, he spotted at least ten witches in pursuit. Cripes! How many were reflections, and how many were witches?

Round the next zigzag, he nearly slammed into a closed door. He grabbed the doorknob. Locked. He whirled to see a big oak door a few feet away. It opened into blackness.

The yawning space looked ready to swallow him whole.

A howl echoed from down the corridor. A chilling, mocking howl.

They were close. Too close.

It was a choice between the devil and the deep, blue sea.

Jesse dived inside the dark room and slammed the door.

"Emma?" he whispered. "Are you in here?"

No reply.

Another wolf-like howl. That didn't sound like witches. What was after him? How would he ever escape?

CHAPTER 12

Jesse fiddled frantically for a way to lock the door.

The howls grew to wild yelps. *Werewolves?*

Like the other door, he found a skull-shaped keyhole but no key. There wasn't time to drag the table across to barricade the door. His pursuers were too close.

He looked around wildly for a weapon. Nothing. Just some books in a bookcase. All options gone, he tensed for a fight.

Wait, he had the flashlight; he'd forgotten to give it to Emma. Body spring-loaded for action, he held it at the ready. When whatever chased him entered, he'd hit it in the eyes with the beam. That would dazzle it and give him a chance to escape.

Thumping footsteps stopped outside the door.

Jesse tensed. Ready or not, this was it.

61

The door swung open.

Jesse shouted, "Get away from me!"

A voice yelled, "Got you!"

What was happening? It was his brother's voice.

Pete stood there laughing so hard he couldn't catch his breath. "Hi, Jesse. What a loser! You should see your face. I bet you peed your pants."

Jesse stared, open-mouthed.

Pete's best friend, his skin covered in white grease-paint, made a chicken-wing movement with his elbows. "Chicken! *Chicken!* Squark! Squark! Squark!"

Pete's cheerleader girlfriend giggled and tossed her

auburn ponytail. "Chicken! Chicken! Squark! Squark! Squark!"

Fury ripped through Jesse. Pete had totally humiliated him. He hated his brother. *Hated him!*

Pete said, "I never knew you could scream like that! You sounded like a little girl. Funniest thing I've ever seen! Right guys? Wait, is that Dad's Brownie camera? And flashlight? Haha, you are in so much trouble." Pete grinned.

Face flaming, Jesse said, "How did you know I was here?"

Pete smirked. "I heard your telephone call to Emma. What a loser! Can't even keep your voice down when you're making sneaky plans."

Pete was really enjoying this.

Pete's friend said, "What a hoot!"

"You should have seen your face," Pete's girlfriend shrieked. "You and your friends, listening to the séance. All goggle-eyed. What twerps!"

"You're all jerks." Jesse glared at Pete.

"How about when he charged across the room?" Pete howled with laughter. "I can't wait to tell my friends. And *yours.*"

"I'll kill you," Jesse yelled. "I'll kill you if you tell anyone!"

Pete snorted. "I'd like to see you try."

Rage and hurt bubbled hot in Jesse's chest. For this; for all those times Pete sat on him and farted in his face; for the wedgies—done hard and mean with Pete's buff arms, all built up from bench presses.

Why couldn't he have a nice brother? Or, even better,

no brother at all. He wished he could squash Pete into a smear on the floor.

His blood pumped hard, and his breath came fast and furious.

With a crazy yell, he launched himself at Pete. His right hand, wrapped around the flashlight, connected hard with his brother's nose.

With a startled look, Pete reeled back.

Jesse reeled back, too, almost as shocked as his brother.

Blood streamed from Pete's nose. "You've done it now!"

Jesse leaped into the dark room and slammed the door. "I hate you!" he shouted. "I hate your guts!"

With a thrill of relief, his fingers found a bolt high up that he hadn't noticed earlier. He slid it fast.

"You're finished!" Pete shouted. "Open up."

"Just leave me alone."

"Fine. We'll end this when you get home."

Pete and his friends' footsteps trailed away.

Shaking from adrenaline, Jesse slumped. He was furious, but he hadn't meant to give his brother a bloody nose. Still, it served Pete right for making him feel like an idiot.

Pete would tell Dad. He'd blab to everyone in town. Jesse would be labeled a loser. The kid who believed in spirits. The kid who fell for the dumbest prank ever.

No one would be interested in Jesse's story of sneaking into the haunted House. Even his pictures would be useless—because Pete's story was better.

Outside the door, Sniffer whined. Oh no! Poor Sniffer

was out there. In all the chaos, he'd failed to notice he'd left his loyal friend behind.

"I'm coming, Sniffer," he called and slid back the bolt.

He reached for the doorknob and found that, on this side, there wasn't one. Just the keyhole with no key.

He tried to pry the heavy oak door open. It wouldn't budge. He must have triggered a spring lock when he slammed it shut. And now he was stuck inside.

What was it about this place and weird doors? The House was like a fat spider crouching in a web, waiting to trap you. No wonder Sarah Winchester wasn't happy. Who would be?

His mind went to Emma and GL. He hoped they'd escaped and were on their way home.

But if not . . . He banged on the door. "Emma! *Emma!* Are you out there? I'm stuck."

Silence.

Then, grudgingly, "Pete? Pete! Let me out. I can't get out!"

He body-slammed the door. Hollered. Kicked. Pounded.

Silence.

Yeah, of course Pete wouldn't help him. He never would. What was the point of having a brother if he was always out to get you? If he was always trying to make you fail?

"Emma," he called, his voice hollow. "Can you hear me?"

Sniffer pawed at the door again. Jesse's chest squeezed. Good old Sniffer, at least he'd stand by him no matter what.

"I'm coming, Sniffer. Don't worry."

Weak moonlight colored everything grey-blue. He fumbled with the flashlight. No go. It didn't work. Pete's big nose had put an end to it. Dad would be furious.

He ran his hands over the walls feeling for light switches. Nothing.

There had to be another way out.

Along one wall, he could just see four fireplaces with stone hearths. This room must be the Hall of Fires. Dad told him Sarah Winchester would light the fires and turn on the vents until the Hall felt like a sauna.

It didn't feel like a sauna now. It felt cold as a tomb.

He opened a set of heavy drapes to let in more moonlight.

Beside a fireplace, he found a narrow door hidden in the paneling. Yes! A secret exit!

It opened . . . to a blank wall.

Well, that was no use.

A thin shadow slid across the ceiling. Something rustled. Something brushed the back of his neck.

"Pete!" he yelled. "I know you're doing this, Pete."

But how could he?

The hair on his arms rose.

Something was wrong.

Get out of here!

Above, a brass chandelier swayed. The lights flickered on, throwing everything into stark focus. Then they went out. On and off, they flickered in blinding flashes. The chandelier swung wildly. He leaped clear.

Too late.

The chandelier crashed down, side-swiping his head.

Thrown backward, Jesse reeled and hit the floor. As crystals and chunks of glass flew across the room, he gasped.

Then, he blacked out.

CHAPTER 13

WINCHESTER HOUSE
THE HALL OF FIRES

Jesse came to, lying on the floor, his skull thumping with an awful headache. That chandelier had hit him good. He felt his scalp gingerly. Something sticky had dried there—blood. A hot lump stuck out like a goose egg.

I'm fine. I'm alive. That's a plus.

He forced himself to sit.

Oh wow, he felt terrible. The whole world spun. He couldn't think straight. He had to get moving, get out, escape.

He hauled himself to his feet. His head reeled.

Something touched the back of his neck. Hands. Icy hands. He whirled around. "Pete!"

The hands pushed hard. Jesse careened across the room. He stumbled against the wall. He couldn't see straight.

Swirling fog poured from all four fireplaces. It materialized into human shapes. Men. Spirits. Whoa. He rubbed his eyes. No way this could be happening. It had to be another trick.

But how could Pete pull off something like this?

The spirits flew at him, mouths opening wide.

"I know it's you, Pete!" he yelled. "Quit doing this. I hate you. You think you're so smart. You think you can make a fool of me. You think you can joke about me to everybody at school. I'll get you. I swear. I don't know how you're doing this, but you'll be sorry!"

Beads of sweat formed on his lip and forehead. His stomach lurched. He clutched at an oak table.

Five misty figures with gaunt faces shrieked, and their mouths stretched even wider. They looked hungry. They would swallow him whole.

No—no, it was a trick!

Breathing hard, Jesse rubbed his eyes.

They were still there.

Spirits!

Ghosts!

The Undead!

He stumbled away from them. Cold sweat soaked his flannel shirt. "I don't believe in you!"

One figure shot forward, materializing right before him. An angry, beak-nosed young man in military uniform.

Jesse kicked out, but his foot made no contact. Instead, it went right through. Dread filled him. "Who are you?"

Matthew. The sound drifted in the air. *Matthew Taylor.*

Matthew didn't look friendly. He looked furious. His eyes, beady above his gaping mouth, drilled into Jesse.

"What do you want, Matthew?" Jesse managed.

You know, boy. Revenge. Revenge!

The others echoed the call, shrieking and howling *Revenge!*

"For what?" Jesse said, but he knew.

I was killed by one of them Winchester rifles. On the twenty-fifth of June 1876.

Jesse's heart rate broke a personal record. "I'm sorry. I'm really sorry." He gulped. Unable to help himself, he asked, "W—who killed you?"

Soldiers. At the Battle of Little Bighorn. I was only eighteen.

The voice broke. Cripes—the spirit was really upset. And who could blame him?

"What happened?"

General Custer led the Seventh Cavalry into battle. Crazy Horse and his braves came galloping at us by the thousands. Those braves were armed with Winchester repeating rifles. We had no chance against a gun like that, one you didn't have to reload. Shot after shot, they mowed us down. We were massacred.

Wow, Matthew was talking about Custer's last stand! Jesse had learned about it in school. "Why didn't the seventh Cavalry have repeating rifles?" he asked, curious despite his terror. "How did the braves get them?"

I don't know. I just know what I saw.

"That's terrible what happened to you, all of you. But in 1876, I wasn't even born."

You're here now, Matthew hissed.

An Indian woman, her white braids swishing, flew at Jesse until her bitter, ravaged face floated inches away.

Those rifles slaughtered herds of Cheyenne buffaloes, she shrieked. *Without the buffaloes, my people starved.*

"That's awful, really, I mean it," Jesse cried and ducked as a third spirit, a haggard man in a filthy, rotting uniform, swooped from the ceiling.

I was nineteen years old, he crooned in a frightening voice. *It was the summer of 1863. The Union soldiers mocked us. Called us graybacks. Lice. They used their cursed Yankee rifle to raze us Confederates down.*

The spirit's mouth was a black hole.

Involuntarily, Jesse jumped back.

I hate you, Winchesters. All of you.

"I'm not a Winchester. I just came inside to take pictures!"

Then, he thought, except Dad works for Sarah Winchester, building stairs that go nowhere to drive the spirits crazy. And Grandpa helped build that weapon. If the spirits find that out, you're as good as dead.

You may not be a Winchester, but you're here. And you understand hatred, boy, the spirit hissed. *You understand it very well.*

"No. No, I don't. War is terrible. Hate is terrible."

I heard you shout, and I know. You hate your brother. Don't you? You hate him.

Jesse froze. "I was mad, but I don't hate him."

He'd said it, though. Right to Pete's face. And then he'd punched him with the flashlight and drew blood.

He was angry, he was hurt, but did he hate him? They were brothers. They used to be inseparable. Somehow, they'd lost their way.

And now this was happening. Had his anger made these spirits appear? Were they drawn by his black thoughts?

Suddenly, he heard a loud rumbling.

It sounded deep down, like underground thunder.

Spirits poured from all four chimneys. They swirled and screeched. The walls shuddered, and the floor shuddered.

Jesse staggered sideways.

Were they going to destroy the whole House? Bring it down, and him along with it?

CHAPTER 14

Winchester House
The Hall Of Fires

Jesse crawled under the massive table as the spirits flew around him in a wild frenzy.

The House shook from side to side. Furniture swayed, and walls vibrated. With an explosion of breaking glass, gilt-framed portraits crashed down.

Jesse dashed from his hiding place, ran to a narrow window, and looked out. He was at least three stories up. Too high to jump.

A man pushing a wheelbarrow staggered across the storm-whipped courtyard below.

Thank goodness. A handyman.

"Help!" Jesse shouted. "Help!"

The handyman didn't hear.

Jesse struggled to open the window, but it was sealed shut. He banged on a glass panel. "Hey!" he shouted. "Hey! You!"

The handyman disappeared. The earth just swallowed him up.

Thick ash and coal dust poured from all four fireplaces. Choking, Jesse rubbed his burning eyes. His head throbbed. He could no longer see the spirits, but his head buzzed with a sound like marching feet. It sounded like an army of spirits marching right at him.

He heard singing. Faint, but growing clearer. Men's voices, singing a marching song:

I wish I was in Dixie, hooray! Hooray!
In Dixie's Land I'll take my stand
To live and die in Dixie.
Away, away, away down south in Dixie.

The rumbling sounded like an approaching freight train. The floor moved; the walls writhed. The ceiling buckled. Whoa! A ceiling board crashed down. Plaster filled the room. Walls creaked and groaned.

All four fireplaces begin to blaze.

Within minutes the room became boiling hot. Clouds of smoke whirled, and he couldn't make out if the spirits were there or not.

Oh man, he never, ever, should have come to this haunted house.

And what was happening to Emma and GL? Had they gotten out?

And what about Sniffer? He could no longer hear his dog. His heart squeezed in agony for his loyal friend.

He went to the door and shouted, "Run, Sniffer. Get out of here, go!"

What if the spirits went after Pete, too? Pete would be clueless about what was going on. What if big, knucklehead Pete had boasted to his girlfriend about how Gramps helped design the Winchester repeating rifle and the spirits heard him? The spirits would demolish him.

"Pete!" he yelled. "Pete! If you can hear me, get away from this house. Run for your life! Fetch Pa!"

Sweating, he dove back under the solid oak table and huddled there. Frantically, he tried to think what to do. The twisting and writhing increased. Would it never, ever stop?

"I'm sorry!" he shouted at the spirits. "I'm sorry you got hurt. But none of us did anything to you. Please, let us go."

CHAPTER 15

WINCHESTER HOUSE
THE HALL OF FIRES

For a moment, the House seemed to stagger and then right itself.

Jesse could hardly believe it. Apologizing had worked!

He crawled out from under the oak table. The awful rocking started up all over again. Ornaments fell from the mantlepieces, and books flew from the bookcases.

When the books were gone, he spotted something, a flaw in the wood paneling beside the third shelf.

Did he dare hope? Could it be . . . a secret door?

Jesse scrambled through the debris, floor surfing as he went. He ran his hands along the paneling, found a button-sized hole, and pushed. A section of shelving moved on creaking hinges.

It *was* a secret door!

He charged through.

What the . . .?

There was nothing under his feet. No floor. Nothing.

He fell.

And fell.

Down.

Down.

"Help!" he screamed.

He was falling—from three stories high. He reached out wildly. His hand connected with something. He grabbed it and held on for dear life.

It was a branch; he'd grabbed onto a branch. Jesse was hanging, swinging, from the limb of a tree.

It's not the fall that kills you, it's the sudden stop. Another of Gramp's not-so-funny sayings.

Jesse choked and began laughing, a hysterical laugh. He'd have to tell Gramps about this.

Beside him, the house still swayed. Below, the earth moved as if a monster snake crawled under it. What was going on out here?

He searched frantically for Pete, Emma, GL, and Sniffer. But there was no one in sight.

The tree branch snapped, taking him with it. He slammed down, landing on his back.

Ow, that hurt. His head hurt even more. At least Dad always said he had a thick skull. He hoped it was true. Jesse moved his fingers and wiggled his toes. Nothing broken. Not so bad.

You'll live. That's what Dad always said. No matter how bad he felt. *You'll live.*

Yeah, he'd like to see Dad handle the spirits and live!

Spots rose in front of his eyes. The grass down here was soft. He'd lie still for a while. Get his head straight.

A chunk of brick thudded to the ground beside him.

Whoa. He sat up again with a start. Adrenaline flared through him.

More bricks thudded down.

Must get away!

Wait, where was the camera? He felt around. Had he dropped it when he fell?

He struggled to his feet, staggered and reeled; the earth was still moving! A sickening sway threw him flat on his face. His outstretched hand closed on a hard, square object. The camera. At least he hadn't lost that. He looked around, trying to get his bearings.

As the ground continued to shake, a slow realization dawned.

He thought about the strange migration of birds and rabbits he'd seen on the way here. He thought about the lurching ground beneath his feet. He thought about the swaying house, the flying bricks, and it all gelled into a single word.

Earthquake.

He couldn't explain the spirits, but deep in his gut, he knew this swaying, thrashing world had nothing to do with them. The ground was shaking because he was in the middle of a massive earthquake!

He stood unsteadily. The sky was growing light.

In the distance, across the brittle orchards and dead strawberry fields, great, gray clouds of dust shot into the air with a massive explosion. Flames whooshed outward, setting the land on fire.

Through his haze of confusion, something told him he had to record this. He balanced the Brownie on a large stone and, winding the knob to advance the frame, he took a picture.

Faintly, but clearly, he heard cries. That sobered him up.

"Emma, GL! Sniffer! Pete!"

What was he doing, standing safely out here? Pete could take care of himself, but Jesse's friends? Emma hadn't even wanted to come here.

He staggered around the perimeter of the house, trying to see into the dark windows.

"Emma!" he shouted. "Sniffer! Come on, boy, where are you? Sniffer! GL?"

In reply came the screams of hundreds of people—but not from the house. They came from the massive building across the fields. They came from The Great Asylum.

Then he saw them, small shadowy figures coming across the fields. Heading toward him, running pell-mell in their dash to escape the Asylum. Some of them were dangerous.

He had to find Emma and the others and get them safely away.

Panting, he stumbled down a path and found himself lost between tall cornstalks. He turned in circles and realized he was inside last year's Hallowe'en corn maze. He loved mazes, but he wasn't good at them. Last Hallowe'en, it had taken him a whole morning to get out of one filled with mirrors and loud buzzers.

Something rustled.

He heard a faint voice. "Jesse?"

Relief filled him. "Emma!"

Jesse pushed through the corn stalks to find his cousin standing there with her big green eyes locked onto his. She looked as frightened as a deer. And why shouldn't she? He probably looked the same.

"Emma!" Jesse whispered. "Where's GL? And Sniffer?"

CHAPTER 16

WINCHESTER HOUSE
THE CORN MAZE

Emma looked ill as she stood staring at him in the corn maze. "I don't know."

Jesse's heart stuttered. He grabbed Emma's arm. "You don't know where GL is? But you were together, I thought—"

"One minute we were running along those corridors, then we got to the basement, and this massive crack opened in the floor. Right at my feet. I nearly fell in, and when I turned around, I saw GL darting back up the stairs. I screamed for him to come back, but he got to the top and disappeared. Before I could go after him, the stairs crashed down. I climbed out the basement window and have been trying to find another way in to get to him. Oh Jesse, what a nightmare. Poor GL!"

"This is my fault. Why did I ever think this was a good idea?" Jesse said. "Did you see Sniffer?"

Tears filled Emma's eyes. "No. Jesse, I was responsible for GL. And I don't even know where the little guy is."

Footsteps crunched on the gravel path.

"Someone's there," Emma whispered. "Maybe it's GL!"

"Stop, wait. I saw people escaping from the Asylum. They might be dangerous."

Despite his throbbing head, Jesse's mind was growing clearer. The fog that had gripped his brain since the chandelier hit him was beginning to lift. He said, "I got us into this, I'll check who's out there."

Commando-style, he crept forward.

Sure enough, it wasn't GL. Or Pete, for that matter.

Instead, a greasy-haired man staggered along the corn maze path wearing a long nightgown and carrying an odd assortment of items: an alarm clock, a trumpet, dress shoes, and suspenders.

The man spoke to himself, crying: "Will he never come? Will he never come with the combination? Oh, why doesn't he come?"

Two men in mud-stained clothing followed on his heels. One yelled, a furious yell. The men were nose-to-nose, like feral dogs.

"You took it," a man with a white Santa Claus beard shouted. "You took it and it's mine. Give it back!"

"No! Never. It's mine now." The second man held a brick above his head with his skinny, tattoo-covered arms. "Come and get it. I dare you."

"I want it!" Santa Claus man howled. "I love it. I love it more than anything."

The tattooed man screeched with laughter. "It's mine. I stole it."

"Give it to me. I love it. Give it to me!"

"No! You can't make me. What are you going to do?"

"I'll bend you till you break."

Yikes! Jesse ducked out of view.

Not fast enough, for a stick flew, arrow-like, nicking his shirtsleeve. Had he been spotted? He sprang to his feet like a stunt man in a Wild West Show and ran back to Emma.

"Quick, they're coming! Run!"

To the north, a great plume of smoke grew blacker.

"Look at the sky," Emma gasped. "Something terrible is happening way over there."

"Oh my gosh. I think San Francisco is on fire!"

"Sure looks like it," Emma said.

Jesse broke through the corn maze wall and found himself back at the Winchester House. A strange yellow light glowed through the windows. Was a fire starting in there, too? The house tilted. The whole building was askew. Hands shaking, barely aware of what he was doing, he raised the camera and snapped a picture. Through the viewfinder, he spotted movement in a window.

His heart clenched. "Someone's in there."

Emma said, "GL? Is it GL?"

"No, too tall. But . . ."

Pete.

Pete, the brother who'd tormented him? Who'd made a fool out of him? Maybe. But he was also the brother he'd looked up to when he was small. And that brother was trapped in a crumbling building.

The Bell Tower leaned, bending at an impossible angle. The bell clanged out an urgent tempo. With a shriek of twisting wood and bricks, the top three stories of the house toppled. Debris slammed down.

Jesse stared aghast. Four stories of the house remained. But how much longer would they stay standing? GL and Sniffer might be in there. Maybe Pete, too. He had to get back in and find them.

A man in a flannel shirt and white trousers, covered

from head to toe in ash, ran across the debris-strewn grounds.

"Help!" the man shouted. "We need help at the Asylum. Everything's gone. The walls. The ceiling. The roof. Patients are escaping. We need help!"

"We can't." Jesse was sprinting, heading toward the house. "We have to find a little boy. He's only four."

The man grabbed Jesse's arm, stopping him in his tracks. The man's blue eyes gleamed. "I saw a little boy. He looked about four. I saw him back there in the fields."

A wave of relief shot through Jesse. "A little boy? Wearing a blue and white sailor suit?"

"Yes!" The man nodded. "That's the one. I saw him."

"Thank goodness," Jesse said. "Quick! Where did you see him?"

"Too late." The man dropped Jesse's arm. "He was eaten by wolves in the strawberry field."

CHAPTER 17

Emma stuttered. "GL was eaten by w-w-wolves?"

Jesse stared, speechless, then dropped to his knees. No. *No!*

More patients staggered across the Winchester House grounds, jumping over downed willow branches. The earth rippled as if some mammoth monster was crawling underneath.

"It's the Kraken," said the man in white. "It lives under California. It's breaking loose tonight."

Jesse's eyes swiveled to him. "The Kraken?"

"Oh yes. The Kraken, boy! Soon, you'll see it. We're doomed. We're all doomed. If the wolves don't get us, the Kraken surely will."

Hands dropping, Jesse got to his feet. "You didn't see a boy, did you? You're lying."

The man laughed. "Choose your poison. Wolf or Kraken?"

"Something's wrong with him," Emma whispered in Jesse's ear.

Jesse agreed. "He's a patient. I bet he didn't see GL at all. I bet GL is still trapped in the house. And Sniffer. If he was out here, Sniffer would have found us. I know he would. I know my dog. Sniffer must be in the house."

"We have to call the police," Emma said.

"We have to go back in before the whole thing comes down," Jesse said. "I'm going to climb up that tree."

Emma shook her head. "We need to find the police."

"Wait, there's that handyman again!" Jesse cried as a dark-haired man rushed around the corner, pushing a wheelbarrow.

"Handyman?" Emma echoed, "Where? I don't see anyone."

"He went that way. He can help, he'll have shovels to dig through the rubble. Come on." Jesse darted after the man.

Emma followed.

"Sir!" he shouted. "We need help! There are people trapped in the house!"

The handyman ignored them.

"Sir!" Jesse ran after him. "Wait!"

"We need your help!" Emma screamed.

"I'm Clyde," the man said, his voice oddly faint. "I'm the handyman."

"That's why we need your help," Jesse called.

Clyde swerved down a side path, shoving the wheelbarrow through mud and ash. He disappeared around a corner.

The friends ran after him.

The handyman had vanished into thin air.

"Where did he go?" Emma said.

"I don't know."

"Are you sure you saw someone?"

"Yes," Jesse said, his head aching.

"Jesse, what if he was . . . a ghost?"

Instead of answering, he said, "We have to find GL and Sniffer."

They stared at one another. Jesse's thoughts raced.

Do you run away from danger, or do you run toward it? Gramps once told him it took real courage to run toward danger.

Out loud, Jesse said, "We have to get back into that house."

She set her jaw. "No. We have to get the police. This is too big for us! What can we do? The police will have tools, they'll know what to do."

Jesse swallowed hard. "But what if it's too late? I have to try, Emma. This is my fault, don't you see that? I can't leave them in there. You go. Run, find help. Your dad and my dad. Tell them to call the police."

Emma nodded. "All right." She grabbed his arm. "Please be careful."

Then she turned and sprinted away.

Jesse took a deep breath. *Ready or not, here I go.*

The Winchester House loomed above him.

Waiting.

Waiting to swallow him up.

CHAPTER 18

WINCHESTER HOUSE
THE HOUSE GROUNDS

Jesse studied the house, searching for a way in. The quickest way would be the fake doorway he fell through.

He caught hold of a swaying branch and swung himself up into the tree. Soon, he reached the top limbs, but the fake doorway was still too far away. Inching carefully along a thin branch, he got closer to the wall. Then he pushed off with his feet and caught hold of the drainpipe. Risky move—the drainpipe was wet. He should have thought of that.

His hands slipped.

Clinging on for dear life, he managed to find a foothold. With a thrill of success, he shimmied upward until he was close to the fake door. With a leap, he flung himself inside, landing face down on the floor.

Puffing, he jumped up. He was back in the Hall of Fires.

Now, though, all was relatively silent. As he stared around, it seemed like the ghosts had been a dream, an awful dream. Maybe it had been. Maybe he'd dreamed it all after the chandelier hit him in the head.

He didn't plan to stay in the Hall of Fires to find out.

The door into the hallway was still locked. He returned to the fake one he'd just climbed through and peered out. The drainpipe continued up past the balcony to the floor above.

Right. Time to start climbing.

He pulled himself, spider-fashion, up the slippery, wet drainpipe. With all his strength, he hauled himself up and over the balcony railing.

Inside the room, dawn light streaked across oak cabinets filled with Winchester repeating rifles, shiny and well-polished. This had to be the Rifle Room. A portrait hung on the wall. A man, a woman, and a baby. The woman was small; she reached just below the man's shoulder. That had to be Sarah Winchester with her husband and child. She wore a gentle expression as she looked at her baby.

Jesse had a sudden longing for his solid, reliable dog.

"Sniffer!" He shouted as loud as he could. "Sniffer. I need you, Sniff. Come on, boy. Where are you, Sniffer?"

From way down the corridor, he heard a woof. His heart leaped. A black shape flew through the open hallway door and into the Rifle Room.

"Sniffer! Good dog, Sniffer. Good dog!" Jesse flung his arms around his dog's neck.

Sniffer was covered with brick dust. But underneath, he had that warm doggy smell. Jesse buried his nose in it. "I love you, Sniffer, you're the best dog ever. Oh, Sniffer. Thank goodness you're not hurt."

Sniffer's tail wagged wildly. He held something in his mouth. Something small and blue. A floppy blue hat. GL's hat.

Jesse grabbed it and held it under Sniffer's nose.

"Fetch GL," he muttered, his voice low and urgent. "Sniffer. Fetch! Fetch! Fetch GL."

Sniffer's dark, doggy eyes lit up—like nothing was so bad that a good game of seek and find wouldn't fix it. He took a deep sniff of the hat, and with an excited bark, he took off.

Jesse followed, almost tripping over Sniffer as he ran in circles around the hallway. Down a corridor, Sniffer charged. He scrambled up a stairway with tiny stairs to a landing. With an eager look back at Jesse, he bolted down a zig-zagging corridor and into a kitchen, a vast room lined with carved wooden cabinets and a big oak table.

He came to a halt, barking with excitement.

A high voice rang out. "Sniffer. Sniffer. Is that you, Sniffer? I want to go home."

"GL?" Jesse shouted.

GL crawled out from under the kitchen table. He buried his head in Sniffer's fur.

The house shuddered again. Yikes! Aftershocks? Another earthquake?

GL shrieked.

Jesse grabbed his hand. "GL! Sniffer found you! Good dog, Sniffer! Come on, we're getting out of this place."

A faint, deep voice rang out. "Help. Help!"

CHAPTER 19

P ete. That sounded like Pete.

"Pete?" Jesse yelled.

"Jesse! Help!"

"Where are you? Pete! Where are you?"

"Help!"

Jesse tensed, and his heart rocketed. His brother sounded frantic.

"Sniffer, find Pete," he said. "Fetch!" He didn't know what else to do. This wasn't a real game of fetch. He had nothing for Sniffer to smell. Could Sniffer find Pete?

Sniffer flashed Jesse an excited doggy look and took off again. With his hand tight around GL's wrist, Jesse followed. As they re-entered the Rifle Room, he saw Pete hanging from the outdoor balcony's railing, trying to climb inside. But something was wrong.

Jesse gaped. What on earth was Pete doing out there?

"Pete!" he yelled.

"This thing's breaking up," Pete shouted. "Help!"

The railing lurched backward, out into space, as Pete thrashed, clinging on for dear life.

"Pete!" Jesse shouted.

A nervous glance showed the problem. The balcony Jesse had climbed onto had pulled away from the house, and the twelve-inch gap at the glass door reminded him how high they were. Pete was about to go plummeting four stories to the ground.

Pete's face was ashen. "Help! My leg, it's stuck."

"Stay still," Jesse shouted.

Jesse dropped onto his stomach. He inched toward the opening grabbed for his brother's hand but couldn't reach it.

If he crawled much farther, his weight could make things worse.

"I can't get my leg out," Pete cried.

The balcony creaked. Swayed.

Jesse tried to ignore the warning sounds and snaked forward. He stretched and locked his hand around Pete's wrist. Chest heaving, he tugged with all his might.

Pete groaned. "It's not working, my leg's trapped. You can't pull me off." He yanked his leg without success. "Just get back, or we're both goners."

The brothers stared into each other's eyes.

"I'm gonna get you off there," Jesse said.

There was a loud crack. Yikes! Iron screws popped. The railing swung into space. Any minute, the whole balcony was going to collapse.

With a desperate surge of strength, Jesse pulled again. Pete, his face red with effort, yanked up his trapped leg and thrust his body forward. They both collapsed through the door and landed in a heap in the Rifle Room.

For a moment, they both lay panting. Then Jesse inched back, tugging Pete's sweaty hand. Inch by inch, they crawled further inside.

"What were you doing out there?" Jesse puffed.

"I came back for you," Pete growled. "This place was falling to pieces, you nincompoop. I came back for you." Pete glared at Jesse. "I didn't want to lose my kid brother. I didn't expect to be nearly killed."

Jesse could hardly believe it.

Pete cleared his throat. "Thanks for having my back."

"I didn't want to lose you either," Jesse said.

A wail came from behind a rifle cabinet.

Pete started. "Who's that?"

"It's GL, we need to get him out of here. Sniffer's here, too." Jesse said. "What about your friends? Are they safe?"

"Yeah. They're long gone. I ran back to the House when the earthquake started. I saw it swaying." Pete glared at him. "Let's get out of here."

A fresh scream rang out. It wasn't GL, and it wasn't Pete or Jesse.

"What's that?" Pete said. "Who else is here?"

"It's probably the spirits," Jesse said.

"Hah!" Pete gave a dry laugh. "Give up on the spirit idea. That was us. There are no spirits."

"I should take you to the Hall of Fires and leave you stuck in there," Jesse said.

The scream came again. "Help me! Help me!"

Pete's eyes widened. "That sounds like a woman."

CHAPTER 20

WINCHESTER HOUSE
THE UPPER CORRIDOR

The scream came again. "Help! Help me! I'm trapped in the Daisy Bedroom. Help!"

"I've been in the Daisy Bedroom," Jesse said. "I think I can find it."

He grabbed GL's hand. The three, followed by Sniffer, charged down the corridor, sliding in brick dust. Rubble blocked the door to the Daisy Bedroom.

From inside, someone shouted, "Help me! My house is crashing down."

"It's Sarah Winchester," Jesse said. "We have to get her out."

"We can't dig through that," Pete said. "We don't even have shovels. We've got to get help."

Jesse nodded. "We can't get to you, Mrs. Winchester," he shouted. "We'll go for help."

"Fetch the police," Sarah Winchester shouted. "I'm trapped! Fetch the police."

SARAH WINCHESTER

"We will." Pete frowned at the winding corridors ahead of them. "Follow me, kiddo."

But it seemed to Jesse that Pete didn't know the way. Jesse looked into Sniffer's bright, doggy eyes. "Home, Sniffer. Home!"

Pete scoffed. "I'm not going to follow a dog. You've got to be kidding."

"Sniffer is smart," GL yelled. "Sniffer knows a lot."

Sniffer led the way downstairs and along zig-zag corridors to the basement. They reached the window and scrambled outside.

"Wow, I'm glad to be out of there!" Jesse said.

"Cripes. Look at the smoke! San Jose is on fire," Pete said. "This must be the biggest earthquake ever."

Jesse stared at the orange sky. "We've got to tell the police about Sarah Winchester."

"Where's Emma?" GL yelled.

"Yes. Where's Emma?" Pete said. "You better not have left our cousin behind."

"Of course, I didn't. She went to get help," Jesse said. "We didn't know where you or GL were. Emma went to get our dads."

"Oh. Well, we've got to get home," Pete said. "Let's go via the city center. We have more chance of finding a policeman there."

Jesse crouched in front of GL. "Come on, GL. I'll give you a ride."

Smoke hung in the air. Although it was morning, the sky was as dark as twilight. With GL on his back, clinging to his neck, Jesse hurried across mud-covered fields and orchards.

They reached First Street. Every building over two stories high had fallen down. Even his school was a flattened mess of rocks and rubble. This was worse than he'd thought. He prayed his parents were alright.

Panting, he rushed down Second Street, jumping over the wild tangle of wires snaking across the road. Telegraph poles had snapped like matches, and the cables shot blue sparks.

His heart thumped fast at the thought of his parents and what might be happening at home. They should have gone there first!

"I don't see any police," Jesse gasped. "We have to get to Mom and Dad."

"Agreed," Pete said, picking up the pace.

In the country lane leading to their house, Jesse saw a horse-drawn fire cart coming to a halt.

He raced to it. Two grim-faced firemen sprayed water at burning cottages. Jesse felt numb. Was his house burning too? He prayed his parents hadn't been hurt.

One of his neighbors stood outside, watching the chaos and holding her cat.

"Mrs. Brennan," he cried. "Have you seen my mom and dad?"

The neighbor shook her head.

Pete ran up to the fire cart. "Officer, we need help."

"Move back, son. Stay away from the horses," the officer shouted.

The two horses reared and tossed their manes.

"Officer," Jesse called. "We passed the Winchester House and heard Mrs. Winchester screaming for help. She's trapped in her Daisy Bedroom."

The gray-haired fireman sighed. "We'll send someone to check that out."

"Winchester House is blocked with rubble, sir," Pete said.

"You'll need crowbars," Jesse said. "And shovels."

"That bad, huh?" The fireman wiped sweat from his face.

At that moment, two familiar figures came running down the road: Dad and Emma. Jesse breathed out with relief.

"Boys!" Jesse's dad shouted. "We've been looking all over for you. We were so worried."

Emma grabbed hold of GL. She gave Jesse a wan smile.

"Dad, we're fine," Jesse said, his heart swelling as his dad caught him and Pete in a hug. "What about Mom?"

"She's fine, too. She'll be glad to see you're safe."

Jesse said, "Mrs. Winchester is trapped in her bedroom. The Bell Tower collapsed. Winchester House is crumbling down."

Dad gasped. "The Bell Tower collapsed? Oh, my heavens!"

The fireman said, "Don't you worry, we're on our way. We'll get her out."

Pete and Dad ran alongside the fire cart. "We'll help."

Watching them, Jesse felt an unexpected surge of pride. What a great picture—he couldn't miss this moment. He pulled the Brownie from his knapsack and took a picture of the firemen, the fire cart, his dad, and Pete.

Then he took a picture of Emma holding GL. "Are you alright, Em?"

"Yes. Thank heavens you saved little GL."

GL, his face red from crying, had one arm around Emma and the other around Sniffer's neck. "Sniffer saved me. Sniffer is my best friend forever."

"You can come and play fetch with him anytime," Jesse said.

"You, me, and Sniffer can be best friends." GL gave a trembling smile. "Because you saved me too."

"That was really brave, what you did, Jesse," Emma said. "You're a good friend. The best."

He didn't know what to say to that. Embarrassed, he said, "I'm just glad you're not mad."

"I never said that," Emma replied, but she was grinning.

"There's just one more thing I have to do." Jesse ran to catch up to his dad and Pete. When they reached the Winchester House, the lower rooms were burning. While Pete grabbed a shovel, Dad helped the fireman unwind the second hose.

"Dad," Jesse said, "I'll do this."

For a moment, his dad looked confused, then he handed over the hose. "Okay, son! Keep it up."

Jesse turned the fire hose on full blast. Whoa. It looked good to see the water dousing the flames.

He made sure to keep the water away from Dad's Kodak Brownie camera hidden in his knapsack. Thank goodness he hadn't lost that. If he had some good pictures, he'd send them to the San Jose News. He'd sign them *Jesse Johnson, Photojournalist.*

His mind lit up as he planned it.

CHAPTER 21

JESSE'S HOUSE
FOUR DAYS LATER

"Jesse! Hey, Jesse, come here."

Jesse ran into the living room. Dad held up the *San Jose Mercury* Sunday newspaper. Jesse's picture of the Bell Tower tilting and about to crumble to the ground was front-page news. What a picture! The dawn highlighted the side of the Bell Tower, just as he'd hoped it would. Perfect!

Page two showed the thick clouds of smoke from The Great Asylum, backed by the glow of the San Francisco fires.

Page three showed the burning buildings, the firemen, and Pete and Dad as they took turns spraying the fires.

"You got a good picture of Pete and me." Dad grinned. "Look at me spraying that hose!"

A short article told how Jesse, Pete, and Emma were passing by the Winchester House, saw the Bell Tower crash down, and called the firemen who saved Sarah Winchester.

The pictures and article were attributed to *Jesse Johnson, Photojournalist.*

Jesse grinned, hardly able to believe he'd made the front page.

"Did you really take these pictures?" Dad said. "Did you write the article?"

Jesse nodded. "Yes, Dad."

With a bemused smile, Dad shook his head. "I don't know what you were up to over there, but well done, son. These pictures are good. Way to go, I'm proud of you, Jesse."

The praise felt so good. Coming from Dad, the praise meant more than anything in the whole world.

Then, Dad said, "You know what a good photojournalist needs?"

Jesse shook his head. "No, Sir." Was he going to get another lecture now?

Dad grinned. "He needs his own Kodak Brownie camera. Seems like you know how to handle it. It's all yours."

"Wow!" Jesse took the camera and wrapped both hands around it. He swallowed hard. "Thanks. This is great, Dad. Thank you."

Emma showed up that afternoon. They hadn't had a chance to tell their friends the whole story. He could hardly wait.

"Are you going to tell them about the scary spirits you saw?" Emma asked.

"Pete says I only saw them because the chandelier hit my head."

"Well . . . it does make for a good story." She grinned at him.

Was Pete right, or had Jesse really seen the spirits? Had he spoken to them? It sure felt like it.

Sarah Winchester thought spirits visited the House. She talked to them every night. What a strange place.

He heaved a huge sigh of relief.

Sniffer nudged Jesse's leg, and he stroked the dog's head. Sniffer had been there—had he seen the spirits, too? Jesse would never know.

Out loud, he said, "You're right. It does make for a good story. But I sure am glad we're out of there."

"Me, too," Emma said. "Wild horses couldn't drag me back there again."

Jesse said, "I have a feeling we're going to be talking about what happened for the rest of our lives. It was touch and go there for a while. But one thing I can say for sure is—we did it. You and me. We went there, we got the pictures to prove it, and we escaped the haunted Winchester House!"

Turn the page
for fascinating facts
about the
Winchester Mystery House!

10 Fast Facts About The Winchester House

1. Has 160 rooms, 40 bedrooms, 6 kitchens, 52 skylights, 4 elevators, 47 fireplaces, 13 bathrooms, and only one working toilet.
2. A door opens to a 15-foot drop into the garden
3. Another door will drop you 8 feet into a kitchen sink.
4. Staircases circle back or lead to the ceiling.
5. Secret passages are found inside cupboards and under trapdoors.
6. A cabinet door opens to 30 more rooms.
7. There are 13 ceiling panels in the entrance hall, and 13 ceiling panels in the greenhouse. Some closets have 13 hooks, and the 13th bathroom has 13 windows.
8. Time Magazine ranked the Winchester House one of the most haunted places in the world, alongside the Amityville House and the Tower of London.
9. Located in San Jose, California, the house with all its oddities and mysteries is open to the public. It's especially popular at Halloween.
10. A designated California historical landmark, the Winchester House is listed on the National Register of Historic Places.

WHO WAS SARAH WINCHESTER?

Sarah Winchester is said to have been a child prodigy, very talented, and beautiful. She married the wealthy gun tycoon William Winchester. When her husband died, she inherited his fortune. It included:

- $20 million in cash (worth around $550 million in 2020)
- Ownership of half of the Winchester Repeating Arms Company, so she earned more money every time a rifle was sold.

WHY DID SHE BUILD SUCH A STRANGE HOUSE?

No one really knows why she built the vast, strange mansion. However, theories abound.

According to popular legend, Sarah Winchester believed she was cursed by the spirits of those killed by the Winchester rifle. She felt that the only way to protect herself was to continually build more rooms in her San Jose home.

Legend also says that Sarah Winchester was overcome with grief at the death of her husband and daughter. She feared vengeful spirits had killed them.

How long did it take to build the house?

Building continued day and night for 38 years until Sarah Winchester's death in 1922. The odd features of the house may be the result of her attempts to confuse and evade the angry spirits.

Before the 1906 earthquake, the house stood seven stories high. Several floors were toppled during the disaster and were never rebuilt.

Did Sarah Winchester hold nightly séances?

A popular myth claims that she held a nightly séance ritual. However, this has never been proven. She was said to have been a reclusive person, and her staff reported she was a kind and generous employer.

The Spirits of the Winchester House

Does the Winchester House deserve its haunted reputation? Are the spirits real? Read on and decide for yourself . . . We've collected 7 spooky facts for you to ponder!

1. Visitors and staff report seeing shadowy shapes resembling people coming around corners and at windows.
2. Footsteps are heard going up stairs when no one is there.

3. Some visitors feel taps on their shoulders, hear sighs and voices, see chandeliers sway, and feel changes in temperature.
4. In 2021 a chandelier swayed continuously for no reason.
5. Many tour guides avoid the corridors of the third floor because of ghostly voices and footsteps.
6. A small entity in dark clothing, thought to be Sarah Winchester, has been heard sighing in the Daisy Bedroom and seen coming down the hallway.
7. The most frequent apparition is Clyde, the handyman, who is seen repairing the fireplace, or pushing a wheelbarrow along a hallway and in the basement.

10 Fast Facts about the 1906 San Francisco Earthquake

Although our story is a fictional tale, it takes place during the actual historical, 1906 San Francisco earthquake. This massive earthquake was one of the largest disasters of its time. Read on to learn all about it.

1. On April 18, 1906, one of the deadliest earthquakes in U.S. history shook San Francisco, California.

2. The earthquake, 7.8 on the Richter scale, killed more than 3,000 people and destroyed 80% of San Francisco.
3. Between 227,000 and 300,000 people were left homeless, forcing them to camp in makeshift tents for years after.
4. The Army, attempting to stop the rapidly spreading fires, destroyed whole city blocks with dynamite.
5. The earthquake caused extensive damage to the surrounding countryside and to San Jose.
6. In San Jose, all brick or stone buildings over 2 stories high were destroyed.
7. San Jose's 3-story high school collapsed.
8. Sarah Winchester was trapped in the Daisy Bedroom and had to be dug out.
9. The Great Asylum for the Insane, about 5 miles from San Jose, collapsed and buried more than 100 patients and medical staff.
10. Witnesses claimed that animals behaved strangely anywhere from weeks to seconds before the earthquake struck.

THANK YOU

We hope you enjoyed this book,
  Dear Reader!
We're always hard at work crafting
  stories with you in mind.
Please consider giving this book
  some stars using Amazon's star
  feature. Your feedback means
  the world to us!

~ Ellie Crowe and Scott Peters

THE I ESCAPED SERIES

I Escaped North Korea!

I Escaped The California Camp Fire

I Escaped The World's Deadliest Shark Attack

I Escaped Amazon River Pirates

I Escaped The Donner Party

I Escaped The Salem Witch Trials

I Escaped Pirates In The Caribbean

I Escaped The Tower of London

I Escaped Egypt's Deadliest Train Disaster

ALSO BY ELLIE CROWE

Surfer of the Century, The Life of Duke Kahanamoku

Nelson Mandela, The Boy Called Troublemaker

ALSO BY SCOTT PETERS

Mystery of the Egyptian Scroll

Mystery of the Egyptian Mummy

JOIN THE I ESCAPED CLUB

Get a free pack of mazes and word finds to print and play!

https://www.subscribepage.com/escapedclub

REFERENCES

Winchester Mystery House, *A Moving Day*, https://www. winchestermysteryhouse.com/a-moving-day, access date 8.2021

Russell, Herbert D*., Lest we Forget. The Complete Story of the San Francisco Horror*, 1906, https://www.mariposare search.net/santaclararesearch/06sanjose.html access date 9.2021

MIT, Edu, *Winchester House*, http://web.mit.edu/al lanmc/www/winchesterhouse.pdf access date 8.2021

Winchester Mystery House, *A Haunted History*, https://www.winchestermysteryhouse.com/sarahs-story, access date 8.2021

Wikipedia, *Agnews Developmental Center*, https://en. wikipedia.org/wiki/Agnews_Developmental_Center access date 9.2021

Made in the USA
Coppell, TX
19 October 2022

84934796R00072